GULITH

Honeymoon In Bedlam

Nelson S. Bond

ISBN: 978-1-63652-298-2

HONEYMOON IN BEDLAM

NELSON S. BOND

I remember the preacher saying, "I now pronounce you man and wife—," and I remember the sweet smile on Lorraine Bowman's face and the dazed smirk on Johnny Larkin's, and the clank of sabers as we walked up the aisle through an arch of gleaming steel. I remember asking to kiss the bride. Then I remember something about a banquet, with somebody passing out drinks, and I remember demanding to kiss the bride again.

Then there was another bottle or three, and it must have been powerful juice because I remember Johnny Larkin frowning when I insisted on kissing the bride. Then I felt sorry for myself and started to cry, and Captain Bowman roared something about, "Take that boiled son-of-a-spacehawk home and pour him into bed," and I looked around, wondering who was tanked, and by golly, they all were but me! Which I tried to explain, standing on a table so I could get their attention, but somebody pulled the table out from under me.

And that's all I remember until I woke up the next morning with my mouth tasting like the inside of a birdcage, and Lt. Sam Evans, Second Mate of the Pegasus, was standing at my bedside grinning at me. Sunbeams were bouncing up and down on my counterpane like elephants. I moaned and said, "Get 'em out of here, Sam!"

He said, "Them? Who?"

"Those little purple men. They're making faces at me."

He said, "Shoo! Go away, little purple men!" and they disappeared. "You," he said, "sure collected yourself a snootful last night."

"Who?" I demanded, holding the top of my head on. "Me? I don't know what you're talking about. Can I help it if I was suddenly taken sick?"

"You were suddenly taken," he chortled, "drunk! I thought

I'd die when you picked Cap Bowman up piggy-back and started sliding down banisters with him. You said you were a space vacuole looking for some place to happen. And when you told the crowd about the time you swiped the skipper's winter drawers and ran 'em up the flagpole—"

"Did I," I shuddered, "tell them that?"

"You sure did. You also had a lot to say about some girl at Mars Central spaceport. You said you called her 'Ginger,' because she was a snap—"

"Go 'way!" I moaned. "Go 'way and let me explode in peace."

Evans grinned. "No can do, Sparks. Bowman sent me down to get you. All brevetmen are to report to the control turret immediately. So grab some breakfast, and—"

"Don't!" I howled.

But I had some breakfast while I dressed: an aspirin, a cup of coffee, and two more aspirins. And I finally reached the control turret of our space-going scow, there to find my shipmates standing around looking very what-the-hell? The skipper scowled at me as I wobbled in.

"Well! So you made it? Darby, there's limits to everything, and you exceeded 'em last night—"

"Look, Skipper," I said, "I can explain everything. It was this way—"

"Best man!" he snorted. "If you was the best man at that weddin', I'm a grampus' tonsils. You was a disgrace to yourself, the *Pegasus*, an' mankind in general—Ah! The top of the mornin' to you, son."

Enter the bridegroom, Johnny Larkin, preceded by a sheepish

grin. He said, "Good morning, folks. Lovely day, isn't it?" Then, to the Old Man, curiously, "I thought they were Earthdocking us for three weeks, Skipper? Why the conference?"

"Your guess is as good as mine. I got a call from G. H. Q. first thing this mornin'. All leaves to be cancelled, they said. We're to have a visitor in a few—There! That must be him now."

It was. Colonel Ira Brophy, one of the igbay otshays of the IPS, the corporation that pays us our monthly insufficient. He bustled in all grins, grunts and glamor, pump-handled the skipper and beamed on us like an overgrown sunbeam.

"A fine looking body of men, Captain Bowman! Yup, yup! And believe me, sir, the IPS is justly proud of this ship and its officers. Yup!"

At my side, Johnny Larkin muttered something that sounded like "—donae ferentes—" But Captain Bowman fell for it, hook, line and sinker. He said, "Thank you, Colonel. And we, in turn, are proud to be privileged to do our little part for the Corporation. Any thing, any time—that's the way we feel about it—"

Brophy pounced gleefully.

"Wonderful, Captain! Marvelous! Yup, yup, yup! I told my associates that would be your attitude. 'The men of the *Pegasus*,' I told them, 'will be delighted to undertake this mission. Even though it may mean the curtailment of a certain amount of personal liberty and pleasure—'"

Bowman's chin hit his wishbone. A pint-sized Aurora Borealis played over his gills. "M-mission?" he gargled.

"Yes, Captain. It is my pleasure to inform you that to the *Pegasus* has been allotted the honor of investigating our recent cosmic visitor, Caltech VI. Yup, yup!

"You will be equipped with motion-picture, meteorological

and analytical devices, and will lift gravs at 19.03 Solar Constant Time tomorrow. I need not assure you that with you go the best wishes of our great organization—"

I didn't hear the rest. I was too busy stifling an impulse to wham Brophy over the conk with a blunt instrument. I glimpsed the pans of Larkin, Evans, Weir, and the rest of the boys, and knew I wasn't alone in my reaction.

This was a hellbuster of an assignment! Caltech VI was the latest addition to Sol's family, a space-wandering planet that, from God-knows-where, had recently swum within the gravitational attraction of our sun—and taken up residence between Mars and the asteroids.

From the beginning it had been a trouble-maker. I needn't tell even the ground-grippingest Earthlubber of you that the solar system is weighed on such a hair-trigger balance that any considerable outside influence will throw it haywire. Caltech VI—named after the old, 200-inch platter that had spotted it—had raised a terrific rumpus settling into an orbit. It had caused howling storms on Mars, ionic disturbances on mighty Jupiter, and blasted a half hundred planetoids clear out of existence.

Astronomers agreed the newcomer could not last very long. A couple thousand years at the most. Inevitably it would be torn to pieces by the titanic tug-o'-war eternally waged by Jupiter and the Sun. But in the meantime, according to the Fraunhofer analysis, there were valuable ores on the interloper. Somebody, the first person or group, who set claim-stakes on Caltech's soil, would clean up big.

Fine, hush? Swell! I should have been joyful at the prospect of dipping into this celestial gravy, eh? But maybe I forgot to mention that already three expeditions had gone out from Earth and one from Venus. All of them had reported successful landings on the planet, then—silence!

Cap Bowman had gathered up his scattered wits, now, and began volleying protests like a skeet-chucker.

"But, Colonel!" he howled, "The *Pegasus* isn't good enough for that sort of job. We're a freighter! Our plates are worn, our hypatomics old-fashioned—"

"Yup," said Brophy agreeably. "We know. But your space record is enviable. You have served the Corporation faithfully and well—"

What he meant was, we could be spared. Johnny Larkin said wryly, "I should think those would be arguments for *not* sending the *Pegasus*."

Brophy glowered at him from behind glinting pince-nez. "And who might this be?"

The skipper said nervously, "Lt. Larkin, sir. My First Mate." He added proudly, "Him an' my daughter had a military weddin' last night."

"That's too bad, Captain," harumphed Brophy. "But to return to the subject—"

"Military!" bellowed the skipper. "Not 'shotgun!'" Then a sudden idea struck him; he adopted a wheedling tone. "Look Colonel—if we gotta go, we gotta go. But I c'n excuse Lt. Larkin from duty, can't I? After all, he's on his furlough. This is his honeymoon—"

Brophy shook his head decisively.

"I'm sorry, Captain. All furloughs are cancelled. All men must report for duty on this special assignment. I might add, though, that if your venture is successful, the Corporation will fittingly reward all participants—"

"An' if it ain't?" asked the Old Man.

"They'll bury us," I piped up, "by remote control. With honors. See you later, boys. I've got to see a carpenter about a coffin." And I left.

So that was that. You don't argue with the I. P. S. The next day found the *Pegasus* loaded to the gunwales with all sorts of equipment. Cameras, spectroscopes, interferometers, gadgets and junk, the very names of most of which were just so much Sanskrit to me. That's where Johnny Larkin came in. He was not only our First Mate; he was our technological expert.

But the Corporation also had the almighty viscera to fill one freight hold with cargo! "Concentrate of zymase," said the lading superintendent. "For deposit at Mars Central on the return trip. Get a receipt from the Medical Officer, Captain."

"What's his name?" demanded the skipper gloomily. "Saint Peter? Oh, hello, son. Sorry I couldn't get you out of this mess. Where's Lorraine?"

"That's all right," said Larkin. "Maybe everything will be all right. She's home. She wanted to come along but I wouldn't let her. Space is no place for a woman."

Bowman growled, "This is a hell of a honeymoon for you, boy! An' for her, too. Well, we might as well lift gravs. Sparks, get clearance from the port."

I said, "Aye, sir!" and did. At 19.03 on the nose we blasted hell-for-Thursday out of Long Island Port, for'rd tubes pointed at a mysterious new dot in the heavens that had already killed more men than a Central American rebellion.

That was at 19.03. At 22.00 sharp, Slops boomed the gong for the late watch mess. And at 22.07, the door of the mess hall opened and in walked—Lorraine Larkin, *nee* Bowman!

Cap Bowman had a mouthful of tomato juice when he laid eyes on her. Two seconds later, his mouth was open in a roar and the tablecloth had a mouthful of tomato juice.

"Lorraine! What in the name of the seven sacred satellites are *you* doing aboard? Don't you know—?"

"Now, Daddy!" She smiled, and my heart did tricks. You've never been smiled at till you've been out in front of one of those extra-special de luxe Lorraine Larkin jobs. She was sugar and spice and everything nice, and don't some guys have all the luck? "Now, Daddy, remember your blood pressure."

"Blood pressure be damned!" frothed Bowman. "You git right off'n this barge an' go back to Earth where you belong!"

"It's cold out there," said Lorraine. "Remember? And besides, this *is* where I belong—isn't it, honey?"

She looked at Johnny Larkin, who was suddenly having trouble with his epi-brothers, dermis and glottis. The first was scarlet, the second was charging up and down in his throat like a berserk elevator. He managed to get a few words out.

"You," he gulped, "shouldn't be here!"

"And where else would a girl be," demanded Lorraine coolly, "than at her husband's side? Especially on her honeymoon?" She plumped herself down beside him. "Bring one more plate, Slops. There's company for dinner."

The skipper rose.

"Enough," he declared, "is too much. I wasn't hot on this trip from the start. Now I'm an Eskimo. Sparks, take a message to Long Island Spaceport. Tell 'em—"

"Tell them," interrupted Lorraine Larkin, "that the captain and crew of the *Pegasus* are on their way to find out what happened to those other poor fellows who tried to land on Caltech VI. And tell them we *will* find out, because we're the toughest, smartest, space-lickingest gang of etherhounds who ever lifted gravs. And there's nothing between here and Procyon that can scare us. Mmmm! What delicious soup—"

That stopped them. That stopped them cold. Bowman looked thoughtful, one gnarled hand caressed his jowls. Larkin stopped trying to talk, a curious look came into his eyes. Tom Anderson's shoulders stiffened; old MacPhee, the Chief Engineer, dragged out a filthy, oil-smeared handkerchief, blew his nose viciously and said, "Grrrumph!"

Me, I was stunned speechless, too. Oh, not because she had reminded me we had a moral obligation to find out what had happened to the previous explorers. It wasn't that she'd roused in me any latent spark of pride in the *Pegasus*, either. What got me was her calling the soup 'delicious'! Good golly, that stuff? Delicious?

So we went on, and Lorraine Larkin went with us. I don't have to tell you about the trip; you can get that from the log book. It was sixteen days to the Mars ecliptic, but Mars wasn't there, of course.

It was sky-hooting along four weeks to sta-board. Little things happened, none important. The outstanding thing about the trip was the dopey way our one time sane and sensible first mate, Johnny Larkin, was behaving.

He had apparently reconciled himself to the idea of Lorraine's being with us. Reconciled? Whoops! He was closer to his bride than twelve o'clock sharp. Everywhere you saw Lorraine, there was Johnny, and vice versa.

Then we hit the highroad between Mars and the asteroids, the great open spaces in which Caltech had taken squatters' rights. Bob Weir punched keys on the astrocalculator and figured it would take us a week and a half to reach our destination. I wasn't sure I could last that long.

For why? One guess. Lt. and Mrs. J. Larkin. Their billing and cooing was enough to make a Martian canal-pussie blush green. Every time you saw Johnny he was playing octopus with Lorraine's hand. He had dawn and soft breezes in his eyes when he looked at her, and the glances she heaved back weren't exactly typhoons at midnight.

The worst part is, they didn't seem to have a bit of shame! They didn't care whether anybody saw them acting like melted cheese sandwiches or not. And oh! what they said! He called her "Lovums"; she called him "Cutsie," which was all wrong, "Bugsie," which was one hundred per cent right, and a lot of other names too nauseating to mention.

But somehow we survived. And finally came the time when the skipper came busting into my turret and bawled, "Git y'r feet off'n the desk, Sparks. Take a message to—"

"I know," I told him. "I already sent it. To Joe Marlowe at Lunar III. Caltech VI is oh-oh under the nose. The *Pegasus* is preparing to land, and the situation is—"

"Ain't you the smart little numbskull?" snorted the skipper. "Remind me to use your brain for mattress stuffin'. No, dimwit, we ain't landin'. I ain't goin' to set down on this here outlaw planet till I learn what I'm landin' on. The *Pegasus* ain't goin' to be number four on the missin' list." He beamed complacently. "Me, I'm smart, I am."

Well, so is sunburn. But who loves it. Anyway, I said, "Well, if we're not going to land on Caltech, what's that big thing looming in the visiplate? Green cheese?"

Bowman took one squint through the perilens and let loose a howl that frightened its own echoes. "He's landin'! The damn fool's settin' us down!"

He made a dive for the door. I grabbed his flying coat-tails long enough to squawk, "Who?" and the answer came Dopplering back, "Larkin! The space-crazy idiot!"

I moved, too. Sheer suction pulled me along as we hit the ramp, charged through the corridors, scrambled up the Jacob's-ladder and bore down on the control room. At the door I managed to pant, "Who—who's in there with him?"

"Who do you think?"

"That's what I thought. What is this? A spaceship or a mushroom?"

Then we were inside, and it was just like I thought it would be. Larkin was seated in the pilot's chair, pushing the buttons that eased the *Pegasus* to terra firma, and hovering over him like a halo around a saint's occipital was his ever-loving bride.

Bowman screamed, "Larkin! Wait!" and Lorraine turned, smiling.

"Isn't he clever, Daddy? He's the best pilot in the whole, wide universe—aren't you, peachie?"

"Now, sweet—" protested Johnny modestly.

"Wait!" squalled the skipper. "Wait!"

"Weight, sir?" said Johnny, lifting out of his daze for a moment. "Aye, sir. If you think best—" And he punched the grav plugs. My knees buckled suddenly as the plates took hold. Bowman stumbled; Lorraine gasped. Over the intercommunicating audio came voices, a dozen irate queries from various parts of the ship. Bowman spoke with an effort.

"Not *weight*, you double-blasted lunatic! *Wait!* Till we see what we're gettin' into—"

But he spoke too late. The grip of the grav plates had done it. Our nose jets spluttered, the ship lurched and slithered, there came a sharp bump, surprisingly yielding and bouncy considering the speed at which we had grounded, and—here we were. On Caltech. Motionless, after weeks of travel.

No, not motionless! For then I felt it. Bowman and Larkin felt it. A squidgy sort of sinking sensation, a sort of wobbling insecurity, as though the ground were opening to let us drop through. The skipper, an incredible mauve color, roared, "Lift 'er up, Johnny! We're gettin' into something!"

Larkin made desperate passes at the control board. The rockets flared and hissed, turning the control room into a bedlam. But nothing happened. I saw why. I yelled,

"We ain't getting—we've got! Look!"

They all stared, like me, at the quartzite forward panes. Blue sky should have been visible through them, warm sunlight should have been flooding the turret. The terrain of Caltech should have stretched before our gaze. But guess again. All we could see was a gooey splatter of *stuff* oozing up the sides of the *Pegasus*. A strange, viscous, colorless matter that surged up and about our ship with weird, tentacular writhings. It covered the entire pane, gulped and burbled sloppily as it engulfed the top of the ship. We continued to experience that sinking feeling—

"Sweet whispering stars!" gasped the skipper. "Am I off my gravs? Do you see what I see? The ground melted an' come up an' et us!"

And I knew, suddenly, what had happened to those who had landed before us on mysterious Caltech. Like us they had been swallowed beneath the soggy, flypaper crust of the alien planet.

Well, everything happened at once, then. I guess I'm just a bug-pounder at heart, after all. My first thought was composed of dots and dashes. I made a bee-line for the radio room, powered the tubes and began CQ-ing up and down the wavelengths like a longhair at the Steinway.

Which was just so much wasted time. I couldn't draw a hum out of the audio. Even the more delicate earphones failed to bring in the powerful Mars-Ceres beam. And if I couldn't get a message in, it's a damn sure thing I couldn't get one out. My transmission was blanked out.

So I hung a sign on my door, OUT TO LUNCH, and went back to the control turret. It looked like the bleacher entrance to Terra Stadium on the opening day of the Interplanetary Series. Everybody and his brother was there. Officers, engineers, blasters, stewards. Even Slops had come up, armed with a rolling pin, to find out what had happened.

As I entered, Johnny Larkin was turning off the hypatomic power, swiveling around to face the skipper.

"No go, Captain. I've tried anti-grav, neg potential and reverse rockets. We can't get loose. We seem to be in something akin to quicksand. Every move we make digs us in a little deeper."

Bowman growled savagely, "If you hadda used common sense instead o' makin' billy-doos with y'r eyes—but this ain't no time to talk about truffles. What do you think? Is this here planet somethin' like Jupiter? Low specific, so we keep fallin' toward the center?"

Johnny said, "I don't believe so. The material about us is peculiar. It seems to be organic. And it has a certain type of inherent energy—"

"Energy?" I yelled. "Hey, then maybe our Ampie can eat us out of here? That little critter can gobble its way through an H-layer. This dish of planetary junket—"

Larkin glanced up sharply. "And just how would you plan to get the Ampie out of the ship, Sparks?"

"Why, through the lug-sail vent, of course."

"No. Don't try that. I have a feeling—"

He stopped. He didn't say what his feeling was. To tell you the truth, the sharpness of his tone made me just a little bit sore. After all, I'm not the dumbest guy afloat in space. I said stiffly, "Then what do we do to get out of here? Or are we number four on the flit parade?"

Johnny swallowed hard. He said, "I'm the tech man on this freighter. All of you clear out of here. I'll find some way—"

His words dwindled into silence. Lorraine looked at him proudly, patted his cheek. She said, "That's right, Cuddlums. You'll get us out, won't you?"

The skipper said, "Gug!" The crowd broke up and began drifting away. Johnny started fussing with instruments and gadgets. Lorraine soothed his brow by tying strands of his hair into lovers'-knots. I got sick at the stomach looking at them after a while, so I left. Cap Bowman beat me to the bar by three drinks—

It must have been an hour later that we felt it. A jarring *whoomp* beneath our keel. The upset-tummy-in-an-elevator sensation stopped. Bowman looked at me and said, "Larkin? He done somethin', maybe?" and we went back to the bridge.

Larkin had not caused the settling, but he was beaming triumphantly anyway. As we charged in, demanding information, he said, "Why, it's very simple. We have finally come to rest on the surface of Caltech."

"Sue me if I'm wrong," said the skipper, "but somehow I got

the impression we landed on this overgrowed custard an hour an' a half ago? Or what's that I see out the ports? A bowl of taffy?"

"No, skipper. We didn't land on the surface before. We landed on a particular kind of matter which is, so far as I have been able to figure out, allied with the peculiar life-form inhabiting this planet."

"Life-form? You mean that stuff's alive?"

"Not exactly. That's the point I haven't been able to solve yet. I've made a careful analysis of the stuff. It seems to be a highly complex carbohydrate. Its formula is C_6—"

"This ain't no time," I broke in, "to discuss mal-demer. What I want to know is, do we or don't we try my idea about putting out the Ampie? Johnny, maybe—"

"No!" he said.

"Well, why not? What have we got to lose?"

"No!" he said again. Oh, all right. I guess he was preoccupied and didn't mean to be curt. But his tone rekindled my anger, and I didn't feel any better when Lorraine said, "Please, Sparks, don't bother Johnny when he's trying to figure this out. Go ahead, sugar-plum."

So sugar-plum went ahead, and I stalked out of the room. I went to my own turret and tried to read a magazine, but I couldn't get interested in the hokey adventures of a Patrolman on Io when I was buried alive in cosmic goo myself. So I fiddled with the dials again for a while. No soap. So pretty soon I got up and looked in my auxiliary cabinet. My Ampie was curled in inside, pale blue and shot full of tiny red sparks, sucking contentedly on an old-flashlight battery. I put on my rubber gloves. I went down to the engine loft.

Ampies live on energy. And Larkin had said the gelatinous mass engulfing us was at least partially composed of energy. Which made what I did seem, to me, quite logical. I pressed the button that extends the lug-sails of a freighter, heard the machinery creak into motion, lifted my Ampie out of its lead-foil container, and shoved it through the widening vent. Then I waited for things to happen.

They did happen! But not what I had expected. I had expected to see the Ampie gnaw a hole through that dough like a St. Bernard working out on a T-bone, rare. But instead, the Ampie touched one shimmering feeler to the mass of gray matter, hummed, sparked, and rolled backward across the room!

I said, "Aw, damn! He was right!" and started to close the lug-vent. But—

It wouldn't close! Because the writhing stickiness was welling into the ship with incredible, fluid swiftness. A heavy, saccharine stench was in the air. Gray streamers fingered toward me. I yelped, slammed tight the engine loft door, and raced for the control turret.

In the middle of the control turret I waited for my breath to catch up with me. Larkin spoke subconsciously from the depths of a deep ponder. "Shh!" he said.

"Shh!" repeated Lorraine. "He's thinking."

"Then tell him to think about pancakes!" I howled. "Because there's a shipful of gray molasses following me up the corridor!"

Larkin started. "What's that?"

I told him. "—it looked like a good idea," I finished, "only it wasn't. Now the stuff's in, and I can't get it out again. It'll fill the whole damned ship—"

But Cap Bowman is no dope. He had already sprung to the audio, was barking orders to other parts of the *Pegasus*.

"Seal port and loft sections of the ship immediately. Lock emergency doors! Get all men into safe sectors!"

Lorraine looked at me worriedly.

"What—what is it, Sparks?"

"Nothing much," I told her grimly, "except that I've just about killed us all. That stuff will ooze through every crack and crevice in the ship, swallow everything just like it swallowed the ship. That's probably what happened to those other explorers. There must have been one dope like me aboard each of them. With a bright idea that—I'm sorry, Mrs. Larkin. I've sure put the final touch on your happy honeymoon."

She was Cap Bowman's daughter; she was the bride of Johnny Larkin. A gal doesn't get to be both of those things without having more innard-stuffings than a sofa-cushion. My words heaved her back on her heels, but only for a fraction of a second. Then, smiling, she turned to Johnny.

"We're not afraid, are we, honey? But you'll have to hurry now."

Larkin pawed his hair frantically.

"I'm doing my best. I've got all the facts. But I still can't quite understand—"

Voices rasped in over the audio. Anderson reported from the sleeping quarters, "All men evacuated, sir. Standing by for further orders." MacPhee snarled defiance from the engine deck, "We've plugged all doors, sirrr! We'll hold this position to the last posseeble minute!"

"It's a form of carbohydrate," mused Larkin aloud. "Plastic. Semi-fluid. But why? Why?"

"Think hard, sugar!" pleaded Lorraine. Larkin said mechanically, "Yes, honey—" Then he stiffened. "Honey!" he said.

I groaned. "This is no time for lovey-dove talk, Johnny!" I cried. "Keep scratching at those gray cells—"

And over the audio, the voice of super-cargo Freddy Harkness.

"Am abandoning holds, Captain. The invading—er—substance has already covered the aft bins and is moving forward rapidly."

"Seal the safety door, Harkness—" began Bowman.

Then Larkin was at his side, suddenly frantic, eager.

"No, Skipper! Tell him to keep them open a minute! I'll be right there. I need three men!"

He lit out for the door. Bowman cried, "No, son—come back! You'll be killed. Come—"

But he was talking to empty air. Johnny was pounding down the runway. Lorraine sniffed once. Then her jaw hardened. She said, "I'm going after him."

Bowman pushed her into a chair—but hard. He said, "You're waiting here! With us. You'll only be in his way. Johnny's the tech man on this ship. If anybody can save us, he's the one." But as her head lowered, his eyes met mine. And the words were written there, "Not this time—"

Still, we had to do something. We couldn't just sit there and take it blind. We had to know what was going on. So we cut in the visiplate to the corridor outside the storage bins. It was a dismal scene that appeared before us.

The long corridor was deserted save for a thin sliver of something oozing out of an adjacent chamber. As we watched, this sliver turned to a bulky, rolling mass; became the doughy body of the mysterious matter in which the *Pegasus* was caught. Like a ponderous wave it surged up the corridor, straining into every crack and crevice, engulfing everything it met.

We saw a tiny, gray ship mouse scurry from under a doorway, hesitate as one pink foot slipped into the sluggish excrescence.

It tugged, trying to get free. But it was like a fly snared on flypaper. It couldn't move. In a few seconds it disappeared. Lorraine began crying softly. I turned away, too sickened to condemn myself again for having loosed this thing amongst us.

Then there were bright gleams in the visiplate, and Johnny, accompanied by three or four not-at-all eager sailors, entered the corridor. As he passed the visiplate, he looked up and grinned at us, nodded encouragingly. Then he ducked into one of the storage bins.

He came out staggering under the load of a heavy, wooden crate. He began ripping the top off this frantically, motioned his assistants to get other similar boxes from the bin and open them. They did so, but one look at their pans told us they didn't like this business nohow!

Finally he had the box open. He tore out a portion of the contents. And—

"Has he gone nuts?" raged Bowman. "That's only that medical junk for Mars! That zy-something extract!"

Johnny made it perfectly clear what he was trying to do. He wrenched the cap off one bottle—and deliberately poured the contents into the nearest pseudopod of the matter now approaching within scant feet of him. Then another bottle; tossed into the mass this time. And another. And another.

Lorraine screamed suddenly, "Daddy, look! He's trapped! Behind him!"

She was right. From another cross-corridor had rolled more of the Caltechian effluvium. It formed a solid barrier through which Johnny and his co-workers could not now escape. They could move neither forward nor backward. In a few minutes the two sluggish tentacles of the syrupy monster would meet. And then—

I said, "Skipper, you'd better turn off the plate."

Bowman nodded. He reached toward the button. Closer and closer, now. In seconds the two walls of matter would coalesce. The sailors had seen their peril. We couldn't hear their voices, but they were apparently pleading with Johnny to let them take refuge in the one, so far untouched, storage vault; seal that door. And he had refused. He was forcing them to hold their ground. All four of them, like himself, were desperately ripping corks from bottles, scattering the medical export into the substance closing in on them.

And then one man slipped! His foot flew from under him, was avidly seized by a tentacle of that slimy mass. His eyes and mouth opened wide; I knew he was screaming.

Larkin stepped forward to grasp his shoulders. The skipper hoarsed, "Look out, son! Behind you!"

It happened all at once. One minute there were two towering walls of fleshy matter surging inexorably down upon the trapped quintet, and the next instant—

The walls collapsed! Just like that! Collapsed into running streams of blotched liquid scum. The sailor's leg slipped free. Johnny toppled over backward into the slippery puddle. A foolish look spread over his face. A look that was mirrored in the faces of his associates. His eyes rolled. He goggled up into the visiplate, kissed his fingers to us, and—and hiccuped! His lips formed a syllable. The syllable was, "*Wheeee!*"

Bowman's shaking fingers sought his jowls. He cried, "My God, he—he's—"

"He's what, Daddy? What?"

"He's as boiled," roared Bowman, "as an owl!"

Some time later—about twelve hours, to be exact—I dragged him back into the control turret. He was still a little blue from the cold shower. But the fog was out of his brain, and that was what was most necessary. For all of us were dying of curiosity.

Bowman said, "Well, your plan worked, son. We got the ship empty, and like you said we would, we pulled out of the goo we was in. Now we're on our way back to tell Earth about Caltech, and—" he added proudly, "—collect that bonus. 'Cause under that scum is a fortune in ores. But what was the scum? An' how did you know you could bust it up with that there zy—zy—"

"—mase," grinned Johnny. "Zymase, Skipper. Why, it wasn't difficult, once Lorraine supplied the key. You might say I was slow in figuring it out mainly because the disaccharose existed on such a gigantic scale that I could net comprehend it."

"The di—which?" I said.

"Sugar," said Johnny, "to you. Or, more accurately, a form of treacle. Honey-gum.

"Here's what I figure. Subsequent investigation may prove me wrong, of course, but my theory must be fundamentally sound or we wouldn't have escaped.

"Caltech VI is apparently inhabited by some sort of gigantic insect, which may be of the bee, the spider, or the ant family. Each of these insects, as you know, possesses the power of secreting fluids which it adapts to its private needs. The ant seals nests and wraps larvae in his, the bee builds hives and makes honey, the spider spins threads wherein to trap its prey.

"We were captured in a gigantic 'trap' built by one of these insects, that's all. From what we saw, I judge that most of Caltech's surface must be covered by these gigantic webs. Miles in extent, hundreds of feet deep. Webs of doom for the unwary. Being highly tensile, gummy, irradiated with a rather unusual form of inherent energy, these traps cannot be damaged by rocket blasts." He shook his head soberly. "I can't help thinking of those poor devils who died there. Like human flies in a monster's viscous web—"

"I can't help thinking of the poor devils who died there. Like human flies in a monstrous viscous web."

I prodded, "Lieutenant, the zymase?"

"Oh, yes. Of course. Well, you know what zymase is, don't you?"

"No," I told him. "Do you?"

"Naturally. A nitrogenous substance. A freshly expressed concentrate of yeast juice. Its action on sugar is to speed up, terrifically, the ordinary process that transpires when sugar and yeast are brought together. In short—*fermentation*!

"As soon as we emptied the zymase concentrate into the flood of honey—for it was that, though I might never have guessed it in time had it not been for you, dear!"

Here he beamed at Lorraine. "—the natural sugar was broken down into carbon dioxide, glycerin, succinic acid, and—er—"

"Urr?" repeated Bowman curiously. "What's that? A new element? Never heard of it."

"And—er—" said Johnny sheepishly, "alcohol! You see, that's why the sailors and I were a trifle—confused—by the atmosphere surrounding us—"

"Confused your hat!" I told him. "You were stewed! But it all makes sense now. The fermentation naturally continued. It loosened up the sticky goo, our blasts dragged us out of the trap. But, say! That alky odor is still all through the ship. We can't air the joint while we're traveling through space. Do you think—?"

But he didn't hear me. For this, after all, was the honeymoon trip of Johnny Larkin. And now, the danger over, he had reverted to type. He and Lorraine looked like a brace of intertwined pretzels.

The skipper coughed. He said, "Sparks? Maybe we—"

I gasped, "Gosh, yes! This red on my face ain't sunburn!"

So, folks, that was that. Oh—one thing more. I was right. That alky odor *didn't* leave the ship. Don't ask me how we ever got back to Long Island Spaceport.

They told me later we zig-zagged in by way of Mercury and Luna. I wouldn't know. It was just one, long, delirious dream to me. I was two weeks coming out of it.

What a headache! What a hangover! What a honeymoon!

www.ingramcontent.com/pod-product-compliance
Lightning Source LLC
Chambersburg PA
CBHW070706280626
47159CB00022B/2308